Clint Faraday Mysteries
#15
A Detour Through Hell

Clint and Judi are going home. They get trapped between two derumbes, along with a busload of people. Then the murder. Could Clint solve this one in the time he had? Hell! Could he keep them all alive in that time!?

Clint Faraday Mysteries
#15
A Detour Through Hell

Contents

About the author

CD was born in Lakeland, Florida. His education is in genetics and botany. He has traveled over much of the world, particularly when he was in music as a rock rhythm guitarist with some well-known bands in the late sixties and early seventies. He has worked as a high steel worker and as a longshoreman, clerk, orchidist, bar owner, salvage yard manager and landscaper – among other things.

CD began writing fiction in 1984 and has more than 100 books published as of this time in SciFi, murder, orchid culture and various other fields.

He now resides in Bocas del Toro and David, Panamá, where he continues research into epiphytic plants. He loves the culture of the indigenous people and counts a majority of his closer friends among that group. Several have "adopted" him as their father. He funds those he can afford through the universities where they have all excelled. "The Indios are very intelligent people, they are simply too poor (in material things and money. Culturally, they are very wealthy) to pursue higher education."

CD loves Panamá and the people. He plans to spend the rest of his life in the paradise that is Panamá

- Estrelita Suarez V.

CD is involved in research of natural cancer cure at this time. It has proven effective in all cases, so far. It is based on a plant that has been in use for thousands of years, is safe, available, and cheap. He has studied botany, and was cured of a serious lymphoma with use of the plant, *Ambrosia peruviana*.

Information about this cure is free on the FaceBook page, Ambrosia peruviana for cancer. CD asks only that all who try it please report on its effectiveness on that group.

A Detour Through Hell

Bad Trip

"Jude, can you see anything ahead through this deluge? I have to creep along up here. These mountains can be deadly in this kind of weather.

"What the hell is going on? They've never had this kind of weather on the Pacific side this time of the year! I'd have never come this way if I knew this would happen! This detour is shorter, but there's nothing for miles!

"Excuse hell out of me if I prattle. Driving in this soup makes me nervous."

"It's from global warming, according to Dave. He says it'll get worse."

Clint Faraday was driving back toward Santiago from Las Tablas with his attractive neighbor in Bocas Town on Isla Colon in the Caribbean, Judi Lum. An unexpected storm caught them in the high mountains. Dave was their nutty musician/botanist/author friend from Bocas Town.

They were a few meters behind a bus, which made them slow down to a safer pace, though Clint didn't take stupid chances when driving.

"You want me to drive?" Judi asked.

"You're damned well a better driver than me, but I know this road. You don't. If I get tired, I'll turn it over to you."

"Okay. I don't think I'd like driving in this. I'm all for stopping somewhere and waiting it out."

"I'm a hundred fifty percent for that! Trouble is, there's not a damned thing for the next fifty or so kilometers."

There was a small mudslide across the road. Clint got out and helped the people in the bus shovel enough away that they could pass. They were headed on, a bit worse for wear and wet, after about twenty minutes. They were perhaps six or eight kilometers farther along when the bus turned on the emergency blinkers and came to a sudden stop. Clint could just see where a section of the road had washed out. He sighed, swore colorfully, and managed to turn the car around to head back the way they'd come.

The little mudslide had become a big mudslide. The road was blocked and impassable. This really brought on some colorful swearing!

He turned around and headed back to where the bus was stopped. He chatted with the driver, who said the road would be repaired on this end faster than behind. The equipment would be brought from near Santiago. They could depend on being there for a day and a half, minimum. Probably two days. He could alert the road repair crew if there was signal up here. Cellulars were worthless. He didn't have a CB, like some of the buses, though it couldn't reach far, if he had one. One thing every one of those people on the bus had done when they found the wash-out was grab their cellular to try to get out. They were all regular types. He wished he had one of those satellite cellulars.

Clint suggested that he tell the people on the bus that they were in for a wait, so conserve food and water, as much as they could. He went back to tell Judy he was glad they had the food they bought in Chitre. They were going to need it. He could give most of it to the people on the bus. He and Judi bought food for a month for them, so it would hold out for a day or so with those people.

"We can use the little stove to cook, but we'll need a dry place. I have two can openers and a package of paper plates. The stuff in the ice chest should be used, first. It won't last when the ice all melts," Judi agreed. "We have a lot of things the natives won't appreciate, though we'll eat like gourmets."

"They'll want the chicken and rice. There's wild otoe, yampi and yuca up here. I have plenty of things, like spaghetti to make soup. There's even a box of chicken bouillon. If anyone's got onions and celery, we can make a heck of a lot of soup that they'll love. There's nothing like otoe for chicken soup. There are blackberries all over the place."

He went to the bus and asked if anyone had any onions or celery. Two Indios said they were taking that to Santiago for the market. They had hundreds of kilos of onions and a lot of celery. They said there was otoe close. There was also probably yuca. They had chayote and plaintains. The Indios would donate it all, even though it was going to market as part of the way they made their living. Clint insisted that everyone would give them a dollar. That would be about half of what they could sell the stuff for, so it wouldn't be too hard on them (he'd pay the difference, no matter how they insisted he not do so. He would tell them he was a rich gringo and it wouldn't hurt him any to help people who were trying to help him). He had chicken and some canned goods and a stove. They would need a dry area to cook the food. They could catch all the rainwater they needed, so it wouldn't be too bad.

Another Indio came to them and said he was taking coffee to Santiago, so they could drink as much as they could drink. He had cacao, too. Clint had packaged sugar and milk in a carton, so that would be well! This one, Eladio Cano, Clint had met in Chiriqui Grande a year or so before. Clint could speak Guayme and Ngobe, though he didn't know much of the language of the Indios on this side of the mountains.

Clint walked around among them. All the women were trying to use the cellulars. There was no signal up here. He warned them they would deplete the batteries and wouldn't be able to call when they were back to a place there was a signal. He came across one man standing away from the others, talking into a satellite phone. He saw Clint and swore, saying there wasn't even a signal for the damned eight hundred dollar phone out here – which was likely. It was below surrounding mountaintops. The angle could make the things as worthless here as the regular phones.

The Indios and Clint started cutting leaves from the large heliconias and strung them on limbs to construct a very dry and secure shelter. The bus driver and some of the passengers pitched in. It was soon done. Judy brought out the little two-burner gas stove and put on a pot of water, the Indios brought their part of the food and an exceptionally good dinner was soon served. The coffee was exceptional quality, the cacao made a good drink for the two six and seven year old children. The bus driver got out a case of beer to drop into the ice-cold little stream (that was now almost a river) running into the washout.

Everyone was in a very good mood and everyone was getting along very well. All of them remarked that this wasn't such a bad thing, after all. Everyone could meet other people and enjoy a little camping trip vacation!

They were going to sack out in the car, Clint in front and Judi in back. It was slightly cramped for sleeping, but not bad. They took some of their stuff to put in the car trunk as the people started going back into the bus. The driver, Sancho Lopez, had rationed the beer. There was enough for everyone who liked beer to have one and two each for

Clint and himself.

Clint said this was really a pleasant way to be detained and started to get into the car when there was a commotion from the bus. A woman was squealing and on the verge of hysteria, so Clint went to see what was wrong.

When she went back to her seat, the fellow who was sitting next to her had gone to sleep, or so she thought, on the whole seat. She shook him to ask him to sit up and he slid onto the floor. There was blood all over! He was dead! There was a knife sticking out of his chest!

"Shit!" Clint said, with deep feeling.

<u>*Do What You Can*</u>

This wasn't the kind of thing you could be prepared for. All he knew was that the suspects were all right here. He hadn't seen any signs of rancor among them. He went back to tell Judi to watch for anything that would give them a clue. A man was murdered on the bus.

He got things explained and a sort of system set up with Judi and went back onto the bus. He showed the papers where he was an agent for the Policia Nacional and said he was going to try to determine who did this. He would need to talk to all of them. Fix in the mind as much as you can remember from the last time the dead man was seen, less than an hour before he was found murdered. Remember who you were with, what you were doing, where.

The dead man's name was Carlos Santamaria Vega. Try to remember if you'd seen him anywhere before this trip. He had Sancho get a list of the names of the passengers on the bus for him with their cedula numbers:

Sancho Lopez M. = driver
Cecilio Pastore = attendant
Carlos Santamaria Vega = victim
Eladio Cano   ind
Luis Silva   ind
Yajaira (Silva) Nunez   ind
Maria Guerra + Nilsa & Juan (children, 7 & 9 yrs.)   pan
Jose Ricardo & Sister Ana   pan
Dona Comacho   pan
Silvestre Mario & Salvador (son 9 yrs.) ind
Arturo Taylor   pan
Carlos Sandros   pan blk
Pacho Sandros (br)   pan blk

Elena Sandros (sis)   pan blk
Guillermo Robinson   pan
Sandy Barnes   NA espa
George Barnes   NA espo
Penny Goodson   eng
Armando Sucha   CR
Pedro Vargas   ind
David Estevez   pan

The Sandros were into real estate. The Barnes and Goodson were backpackers/surfers/tourists. Taylor worked for IDAAN (the water agency of Panamá in Santa Lucia – that Clint never heard of). Vargas owned a pescado supply company in Pedrigal. Estevez was a lawyer. (*Him!* Clint thought. He didn't like most of the Panamanian lawyers, even a little bit. 90% of them were worse crooks that the ones they were defending). The rest didn't give information and Sancho didn't ask.

Clint asked Sancho to have Cecilio bring everything Santamaria had as baggage to him. He had an electric lantern that would hold out well until dawn, as well as several flashlights. No one wanted to stay on the bus, except the Indios, who were perfectly well aware that people died from many things. A dead body the first night wouldn't stink or anything. They threw a plastic tarp over the body and went to sleep in their seats in the rear of the bus. The body was in the second seat back from the door on the right. Judi grinned at the practicality of the Indios. The rest would sit around outside in tarps hung over limbs to keep them out of the drizzle. Clint wondered what they would do if another heavy deluge-type band came through.

One woman, Maria Guerra, said there was a row of conduits about half a kilometer back that were plenty big for sleeping. She would take her children and go back there. Most of the others thought that was a good idea. One other noted the conduit. She said they were meter and a half diameter and about six meters long and there were twenty or more of them. That was plenty of room for three or four busloads of people. They would have to be careful that there weren't any dangerous snakes or spiders in them.

Clint suggested Sancho lock the bus and that everyone go to the conduit pipes for the night. Take only what they needed and leave the rest locked up. Sancho said Cecilio would stay with the bus. He would have more than enough comfortable room under the cooking shelter.

They formed a parade of sorts and went there. Clint drove back with his lanterns and such and shined his headlights into the conduits that were at angles to be in them. They used flashlights to check out the other tubes. They found a dangerous spider in one, but nothing else dangerous.

Everyone chose a spot and moved in. Clint and Sancho made a tent of a tarp carried on the bus to cover luggage on the top. Seeing as there were only surfboards and some fresh vegetables up there, they used the small tarp for that and the large one for the tent. Judi said she'd take notes and they could wake anyone needed up for the few minutes of questioning.

Clint took the children first, together. He only wanted to know if they heard anyone arguing or saw anyone doing anything that didn't seem right. They hadn't. They had been with their mother/father the whole time. That would probably help eliminate those from the suspect list.

He decided to take the Indios, next. Only one of them had any possible motive that Clint could see. They were a nonviolent people. They were together, the Cano/Silva trio. The only time they were apart at all was when they were getting the vegetables to cook. Silvestre and his son were with them all the time.

Next was the Sandros trio. Together all the time.

Jose and Ana Ricardo were together the whole time. The Barnes and Goodson were together the whole time.

His suspect list, serious suspects, was growing shorter. Sancho was driving, then with Clint with the food. Cecilio was with Clint and Judi that whole time, working on the food.

The rest would wait until morning. Clint wanted a clear view of their facial expressions and body language when he asked his questions. He would spend awhile thoroughly going through Santamaria's luggage. There was a large maleta and a briefcase/laptop case.

With no laptop? There wasn't anything in the laptop side except two memory sticks that were in with the papers on the briefcase side, along with two cellulars, one Movistar and one Mas Movil, with chargers for them.

Clothes, shaving kit and such, extra shoes – totally ordinary.

Clint looked through the papers. Not much to tell him anything, unless he knew what to look for. There wasn't a note about being threatened or anything. Most of it was standard stuff that might be carried by any businessman.

Santamaria had been a supplier to hardware stores. Painting and gluing materials and tools, with a sideline of making signs of all types. He apparently had a small shop for that in Santiago. He lived close to Santiago on a finca that he rented out to some cattle ranchers for pasture. He supplied in Chitre, Las Tablas and all the towns on the peninsula and back toward Santiago. He had orders from Las Tablas, Chitre and Piedasi this trip.

Cecilio said he remembered that he got on the bus on the corner after the terminal as it left. He had put his maleta under the seat and left a small wrapped package there to reserve the seat, then had arranged for the bus to pick him up there because he had to meet a business cita (date). That could mean a lot. If someone was following him and saw him getting the bus, they could get in a seat behind and have a newspaper or something hiding them when he boarded later. He could have suspected that he was being followed and arranged getting on the bus a block from the terminal so a follower wouldn't be able to catch the same bus. That would mean he expected some kind of attack – or something. He should have left ... maybe he did! That computer was gone!

Clint could only hope the memory sticks were deliberately put in the briefcase section of the case, so taking the ones stored with the computer wouldn't give the taker the information he/she was taking it to hide.

Clint decided to wait until morning to look further. He was getting an idea about where to look.

He thought a moment, then woke Sancho and said to very quietly come with him to the bus. There was something there they had to find.

Cecilio was there with the keys to the bus and would know where every little thing that was out of place should be. That was part of his job.

The computer was easy to find. It had the running light on and the low battery light on. It was under the seat behind the driver. It was running a program. "Format Hard Drive." There had been something on that computer the killer thought must not be found. He could hope it was also on one of the memory sticks.

There was a camera download cord under the seat. Was

it a picture? Where was the camera?

They searched the bus. No camera under a seat or whatever.

Did that mean the killer had that camera? All he/she would have to do is format the memory. Surely the camera wasn't thrown out the window or such.

That would mean the killer also still had those memory sticks. Throwing them out the window would be too dangerous. Anyone finding them would automatically run them to see what was there. That was two things that would possibly identify the killer.

Sancho called Clint from halfway back in the bus. He found six memory sticks stuffed in the seam in back of the seatpads of two seats. He handed them to Clint.

Well, there were probably no prints on them, anyway.

They didn't find the camera. Clint took the memory sticks back and plugged them into the USB ports on his laptop. They were formatted. The killer thought of that, so the camera would be formatted, too. All finding it would do is identify the killer – if they could even prove it was Santamaria's camera. He didn't even know the brand of the camera.

Shit!

He and Sancho went back to the camp in the culverts. It would have to wait for morning – about two hours away.

Clint had waited to look at those memory sticks from the case until he had a hint of what to look for. He did that while Judi and the women were preparing breakfast. They had flour and oil and everything else they needed. The Indio women knew how to make excellent hojaldres and tortillas they served with boiled eggs. Judi had made deviled eggs out of part of the eggs. Some of the Panamanians wouldn't eat them when they were told they were huevos diablos, translated to mean "the eggs of the devil." The Indios grinned at her. That meant more for them. They believed that any "devil" who existed was inside a person, not someone who would torment their souls for eternity as a reward for worshiping him. They found the concept ridiculous to the point it was silly. The idea of hell was as silly. Hell was also inside a person.

"Not true!" Judi said, grinning. "This is a detour through hell right here!"

"Only for some," Yajaira replied, eyes sparkling and with a laugh in her voice. "Some find it a good time for most where we get to know other people. The gringas are very nice. We are a curiosity for them. They don't understand us, but we don't understand them, so it's equal!"

Clint grinned when he overheard that. This really was a detour through hell for Judi and most of the Panamanians. It wasn't, particularly, for him, now that the rain was lessening, and it certainly wasn't for the Indios. He had a mystery to solve and only until the road was opened to solve it. He hoped to have it solved before darkness tonight.

He looked around at the group. More than half of them were up for coffee and hojaldres. The Indio kid was up with his father and drank a cup of the strong coffee they liked with them. He was ready to go to work, as usual. He had his duties and chores since he was about six years of age and would have a strong work ethic for the rest of his life, as a result. It was part of their culture. Everyone worked cooperatively for the family and community.

A large truck was heard in the distance, so the equipment to repair the road was on its way. Clint went to his laptop and turned it on. He would wait until after breakfast to interview the rest of them.

The first memory stick was just business. He scanned pages of invoices and such, without finding anything special. There were no pictures-as-pictures in the memory, though there were product pictures and so forth as PDF files.

The second stick had a couple of pages that were in code among the business items. There were several pictures, but nothing in the least out of the ordinary. They were of stores and fincas, with two of a waterfall from across a valley. Clint had seen that fall.

This was nothing. Clint stopped with the cursor over a picture icon. A script came on the screen beside the arrow: 14-4-11, 10:50AM, Olympus 850.

He was in luck, in one way – an Olympus Stylus 850 was a special camera that could be used underwater. There was no way two such cameras would be on that bus. The odds against that were tremendous.

Clint did have one thing he could do, now. He could find that camera if he had to search every item in that bus. He had the authority, as an agent for the police here in Panamá. It would be fun listening to an explanation of why a person would have that kind of camera – unless it was the tourists. Surfers carried that kind of camera, sometimes, though it wouldn't be likely it was the same model.

They were sitting on a culvert, eating breakfast. He decided to eliminate them, first thing, though he never had a serious thought they would be involved.

He asked them if they carried cameras. They did. He said he would like to borrow one to use for pictures of the crime scene and so forth.

Goodson went to her backpack and handed him – an Olympus Stylus 850.

Shit!

He hit the memory button and saw scenes from weeks back. More than a hundred shots, though the 850 would record a thousand shots before you had to empty it. He remarked that it was a really good camera.

"I have one," Sandy Barnes said. "A lot of us water players have them. They're pretty good."

She said hers was on the bus, which wasn't smart. She should have thought to bring it or it could disappear.

Odds of two such cameras on one bus in the middle of nowhere were beyond calculating, at least to Clint. There were three here. Clint shook his head and said he was going to take a few pictures of the scene and would be right back. Half an hour. He would bring Sandy's camera back, if she liked. She would.

He went to the bus and did take pictures of everything. He should have thought of that from the first. He had a camera and Judi had one. He had to take some with this camera for cover when he asked about other cameras.

He checked out the luggage that was still on the bus. There wasn't much, so the killer had taken the camera to the culverts.

He went back to hand Sandy her pack and to download all the pictures he'd taken from her camera. She asked that he leave them in the memory for her own memories.

Everyone was up and about, except Armando Sucha. It was almost eight o'clock. Where was he?

Several people went to look into all the culverts. Pacho Sandros called that he found him. He was dead. His throat was cut.

This was getting out of hand! Sancho had put that Sucha was from Costa Rica on the list. It wasn't so bad when this was limited to a small area, but did this mean something about it reached into Costa Rica? Costa Rica was a long way from this area.

Clint sighed and said everyone was to come to the kitchen area, where they were to stay together. Period. They were to bring their luggage and were to keep a solid grip on it. One of them would have a hell of a lot to explain before this was over.

Everyone was willing to cooperate. The Indios and the tourists were together most of the time, already, and had a sort of rapport developed. They were interested in each other.

They all put their luggage on the top of the culverts, in plain sight. No one objected or resisted in any way, so Clint knew the camera was somehow disposed of. It would be gone – but how? When?

When the killing here was done. That put a severe limit on where it could be.

Clint could trust the Indios, except Vargas. He didn't know anything about him and he didn't hang around the rest of the Indios. The way they stuck together meant that left a couple of very important questions to be answered.

He would call each one and they would bring him the luggage. He would look through it and ask a couple of questions.

Maria Guerra was first. She didn't know much of anything. She kept most of her attention on her children. This was not a good thing for children to be exposed to. It was horrible! There was nothing – like a camera – in her luggage.

Jose and Ana Ricardo were going to Panamá City to shop and visit her grandmother, who lived there. There was nothing in their luggage, but that gave Clint an idea that could be important. Jose was from Divisa and Ana was originally from Panamá City, but had lived in Las Tablas for nine years before she married Jose three years ago and moved to Divisa. They took the Las Tablas bus because they went there to buy a gift for her grandmother.

Dona Comacho was from Bugaba, She was in Las Tablas for a vacation and was going home. She was a teller at Global Bank. There was a camera in her luggage, but it was a Maxell.

Arturo Taylor was more a solitary type. He was from Piedasi for the past three years, and from Santiago before that. He was going to Santiago to visit his brother on the farm they co-owned there. He had worked for IDAAN for ten years. He had a Look camera in his case. Nothing else of interest. He had gone to breakfast about six. He didn't see anyone or anything out of the ordinary.

The Sandros family were from Colon and were there to try to find a place to move to. They hated Colon and its crime. It was dangerous to even walk down the street, anymore. They weren't wanted anywhere. As soon as they mentioned Colon, people turned to ice toward them.

Clint knew how that was. Colon has such a bad

reputation that people will become suspicious if you're from there. Blacks had it really hard. There were plenty of good, decent people among them, but they had to live with the reputation the criminal types established. Clint suggested they try Bocas. They'd come to that conclusion, already, and would go there next. There was the usual among their luggage, plus a little bag of pot. Clint grinned at Pacho and put it back. Pacho giggled. They had two cameras. A Kodak and a Look.

Guillermo Robinson was from Arenas, on the other side of the peninsula. He was in Las Tablas to see a man who wanted to buy his large finca on the seashore, there. He would go to Santiago for the papers and plano for his property and the certification, then would go back to Las Tablas. His luggage was normal – except for an Olympus Stylus 850 wrapped in a blue bandana. When Clint pulled it out, Robinson cried, "That isn't mine! How did it get there?!"

Clint questioned him carefully. He had been up since about six fifteen, had used the rocks down by the stream for a restroom, had met with Jose and Ana for breakfast. His maleta was in the culvert, where he slept. He was the only one in it. He couldn't sleep if there was anyone else there. Several were like that. Anyone could have put the camera in his maleta. Shit!

Pedro Vargas was Indio, but wasn't very well accepted by many of them because he was working in a white man's job and doing very well with it. He was from Santa Fe and was on his way home. His luggage was normal, though Clint felt he already had the camera and that it was a dead end clue.

There was one thing Clint saw as soon as the maleta was opened. There was a charger for the special batteries used only in the Olympus Stylus cameras. Vargas had no idea of how it got there. He was another who got up early and left the maleta in the culvert where he slept. The only other person in that culvert was Arturo Taylor, and he was up early, too.

David Estevez was a real estate agent from El Valle. He had lived in Panamá City for the past eleven years. He went to University there, then worked for a broker, then went into business for himself. He was in Chitre to consult with a broker there about a large seaside finca for sale.

"Near Chitre?"

"No. Pocri. It isn't that far, but can't be called Chitre."

Clint knew Pocri. He nodded. There was nothing of interest in his luggage. Pocri wasn't seaside, but was connected, in a way.

That was his crop of suspects. Nowhere else to look, so get at finding something here. The internet connection wouldn't work there, as the cellulars wouldn't work there.

Clint thought for a few minutes. He didn't have anything to hang anything on. Personality didn't give him a clue. He had to find what the killings were about. What connected the two victims and someone else?

There was that code. Two pages of code. It could hold all the answers, or none. He didn't know if that was connected, in any way. The pictures didn't show much. There were seven.

The waterfalls. Clint had stood close to where those pictures were taken and had several pictures very much the same that he had taken. The finca pictures could well be of that finca from which the waterfall pictures were taken. It was a very large finca and was for sale. Manny was considering buying it.

David Estevez was a real estate agent/broker.

There was the back end of a car showing in the picture of the gate to the finca. It appeared to be a black Mitsubishi with a sticker of some sort on the bumper and another one in the rear window. Nothing out of the ordinary. Probably the car Santamaria drove there in ... then why take the bus here? That wasn't quite in sync with anything he could think of – so it was probably someone else's car. Someone who took him to see the finca. It wouldn't be Estevez's car. He wouldn't be on this bus.

The other pictures: Gran Fereteria Martin. A medium-sized hardware store. Four cars out front.

Centro Supplies. Another much like the first. Two cars out front and a truck.

Almacen Florita. Same. Two cars out front. Clint was moving to the next when he went back.

There was a black Mitsubishi with stickers. It was the same car. If he was using that car or was being chauffeured around in it, that would be why it was in only two pictures. Not enough. It could be in any of those pictures. Logically.

Two more, then Santamaria standing in the door of a Datsun small pickup 4X4. There was an attractive woman across, behind the wheel. The next picture had that truck in it with him and the woman standing beside it in front of another hardware store.

Apparently, that was the transportation he was using. The black Mitsubishi suddenly became important. It was in one more picture, apparently, the last taken with that camera on that date. It was a picture of the Mitsubishi with a tall gringo-looking man and a fat black man looking at some papers that were spread out on the hood. There was a third person in the picture, but he was back and to the side and wasn't in focus well enough to identify, other than that he was average.

Clint felt that man was the important one here. He also felt he could find out who that man was by tracing that car. The license plate was only partly visible in the first. Other than that it was a Panamanian plate, nothing. The second was worse. The third showed the plate started with 542. That was all.

He could find a black Mitsubishi with two stickers in specific places and with a Panamanian license plate that began with 542 and trace everything else back from that. He hadn't the least doubt he could solve this within hours, when he got back – to Chitre.

He didn't want to wait. Two were dead, already. That was two too many.

Judi came in to tell Clint she had the Indio women

looking for anything they could find. One of them was washing clothes in the stream and found a knife. She hadn't touched it. She would show Clint where it was.

That would be the murder weapon. They had the first. It was sticking in Santamaria's chest.

Santamaria had met with someone on this bus and had learned something. What? That it was incriminating was a given.

Someone else on this bus met with the killer – and probably Santamaria.

Then Santamaria would have spoken with him or her on the bus. It was agreed that he didn't seem to know anyone there.

Damn it! What the *hell* was the connection with Sucha? Sucha didn't seem to know anyone else on the bus, either. There had to be a connection.

Maybe the connection was that Sucha saw something? That seemed the most logical answer.

It still came back to that car.

Clint knew a little about breaking simple codes. If this was just a substitution code, that would possibly work fairly well. He had nothing much else to do, so would spend a little time on it. It was a number code. Those were the easiest to break.

He copied the pages and turned off the comp. No sense in killing the batteries. He had the first paragraph to work on..

The highest number was 34. It was only used once. There were series of from one to nine numbers, then a double space between, so those would be words. The most common two were 2 and 28. There were words that ended in both. It was Spanish, if that's all Santamaria spoke. A and O. Both were used alone. 16 was used alone, though not very often. That was most likely Y.

Clint took the laptop from under the bus seat out to look over. It had an English keyboard. It wouldn't have certain symbols used in Spanish, such as the accent mark used in such words as Panamá. That could be important.

He stared at the keyboard. A was the first letter on the second line. Did that mean ... no. It was used alone, so line number on the keyboard didn't mean much.

He counted in every way he could think of. A was the second letter if you went from top left downward as the keys lay.

Y was number 16, by that system. It fit. O was #28. The code was something he came up with fast, so it was easy to break it fast. He could now read the pages.

Investigacion finca por Williams. Esta grande con vista magnifico del mar. Tiene una poco problema con DDP. Cuestion contra plano. Posiblemente hay problemas con aplicacion por titulo. Hay cuidado!

(My investigation of the land for Williams. It is large with a magnificent view of the sea. I have a problem with the ROP. There is a question against the site plan. There will possibly be problems with any application for a title. Take care!)

The second stated: *There was a man from the agency who was supposed to be a thief who worked with thieves. The land is there and it is real. It is doubtful that a title will be issued for that land until many questions are answered. There may be several who claim to own it. It is from a long time ago when there were not good records kept of such land that no use for could be found at that time. It was not accessible and there could be no certain way to survey there. My recommendation is to seek land elsewhere unless a government guarantee can be obtained. I will find the names of the persons doing this that Mr. Williams can use to bring investigation against.*

That person was on this bus. There was one real estate person on the bus. Estevez. He was a lawyer, and lawyers here are famous for being the worst kinds of crooks. (Really! As bad as or worse than the states!)

Clint knew better than to concentrate totally on a single suspect in a murder case, regardless of his personal opinion. Estevez was a prime suspect, but not the only suspect. He would be on the bus because Santamaria was on the bus. If he drove a black Mitsubishi with two stickers in specific places and a Panamanian plate that began with 542, he would concentrate *almost* exclusively on him. He had been burned with sure things enough in the past to know better than to ever take anything as 100%.

His next step was ... what?

Opportunity. Okay, he probably had that. All of them, with the noted exceptions, did.

Didn't they?

Santamaria had been dead less than an hour, when found. That established a very short period of time when the murder could have taken place. From what Clint knew about fixing the time of death, Sucha hadn't been dead much longer than three hours. Probably closer to two. Learn who had opportunity from four thirty until six thirty. Anyone near that culvert back there would be noted when anyone went back that way.

Clint called them all together and asked that they establish where they were from four thirty until about six thirty.

Guerra was with her children. Dona Comacho was in the same culvert and would know if anyone left from the front. The children would know if anyone left from the rear, though it could be easy to see prints or whatever if anyone looked back there. It was muddy.

Jose and Ana were together. Neither could have left the other didn't know about. Everyone was skittish and woke up at the least noise. The Indios, except Vargas, were together. No one left the culvert.

The Sandros family were together. No one came or went.

The gringos were out of it.

Dona could have left. It was just possible.

Arturo Taylor could have left.

Guillermo Robinson could have left.

Pedro Vargas could have left.

David Estevez could have left.

Five out of twenty. It was drawing in.

Salvador Mario said Vargas did not leave his culvert. He could see it from where he was and he didn't sleep after about two o'clock, when his father came. He had plenty of sleep and felt it would be better if one of them stayed awake to watch. Sancho Lopez said he could see Salvador in the end of the culvert most of the night. He didn't sleep, either. This was on his bus and he was horrified about it and couldn't sleep. He wished he had saved a beer, because that would let him sleep a little.

Four out of twenty.

He thought about things, then decided to try something else. He asked how many of them could drive, had licenses. Panamanians. He wasn't about to let a foreigner use his car, in a case like this. The police would harass the hell out of them if they were stopped. Judi raised an eyebrow, but didn't say anything. She knew Clint had something in mind. Sancho and Cecilio had to stay with the bus.

Maria Guerra, Jose Ricardo, all the Sandros, Guillermo Robinson and David Estevez drove. Taylor was probably out. Three out of twenty. His prime suspect was still in it. The noose was drawing closed.

How trite!

Clint needed a way to eliminate two of three. He could probably put Dona out of it. Robinson and Estevez were his real suspects – and he didn't see Robinson as a killer. Trouble was, he couldn't see Estevez as a killer, either. As much as he wanted it to be him, as sure as he was, personally, he didn't see it. There was something missing.

Judi got him aside and asked what that was about. Clint explained about his theory that someone driving a car was neck deep in it. He could describe the car, all he had to do was connect one of them to it. She said she'd find out if any of them had a black Mitsubishi.

Clint was talking with Sancho a few minutes later and asked if he had a way to find who owned a black Mitsubishi with a sticker in the window and one on the bumper that had a Panamanian license plate that started 542.

"Not out here. Five minutes in Chitre," he replied. "What kind of stickers?"

"I couldn't read them in the pictures."

"What colors?"

"Green and a sort of bronzy color, with black letters."

"Black letters that said Hertz? It was a rented car. The driver should have the return receipt with him."

"Oh, shit! Sucha had a receipt for a rented car! I saw it in his wallet!"

He went to his car, unlocked the trunk and took out the box of evidence for Sucha. There was a receipt in his wallet for a 2009 Mitsubishi 2 door sedan. He turned it in just before getting on the bus.

"What the unholy *hell* is going on here?!" Clint demanded. "That would mean that he killed Santamaria, now someone's killed *him*! Do we have two murderers on this bus?"

"I hope sincerely not! One is too many!" Sancho cried.

"Now I'm not even sure I'm looking in the right place for motive. This is *not* anything like I was thinking.

"Or is it?"

He went back to his car. Judy said she hadn't found anyone who noted any of the others in a car at any time. He said he found who had the car. Sucha.

"What does that add to your case?"

"It adds zilch! It destroys part of what I was trying to prove or disprove. It makes part of it irrelevant. This is one of those one step forward and two back deals."

"I'm getting a bit worried, now," she replied. "When it was something you could maybe understand, it wasn't so scary. Now we have some nutcase who's killing people and it's someone we all know who can pose as a regular person.

"Clint, I know you'll argue, but it has to be the people from Colon. This is getting to be a regular scene there – and they're the only alibis they have. If they're in it together, they'll naturally back each other up with the same rehearsed story."

Clint nodded slowly. That was something he'd considered. He wanted to reject that it may be more than one.

There wasn't much to do. He did remember what was said about going out the back end of the culverts. It was muddy there. It would keep footprints for months. All of them ended in that mud pit.

He climbed on top and went to the end. There were no footprints back there. At all.

He noted that he could grab the top and swing up with a little effort. It would be a lot easier to go back down from up there.

Would anyone note seeing somebody on top? Was anyone ever looking up there?

One person might. He went to ask Salvador if he saw anyone on top of the pipes at all during the night.

No, but he could only see the front ends. The back ends were behind and he couldn't see through the pipes.

Well, he knew a minimum amount about something indefinable. He could use a cup of coffee about now.

Judi came in to say that Nilsa, the daughter of Maria, said she heard some animals during the night. She thought it was wild animals. They were bleating about something. It was like dogs barking, but it wasn't dogs and it wasn't barking. She just didn't know whether it was earlier or later.

Clint thought, then went back to Salvador to ask if he'd heard the animals. When was it? Early or late?

"Early in the morning and late at night. Both. Monkeys. They make noises all night."

"Oh. Howler monkeys."

"Whiteface monkeys, too. The Whiteface are not so noisy at night. Only twice last night. Perhaps two hours before the light. It was their call that there is a snake. It is more high and more long. It was not too close."

Like a bleat. Four o'clock or thereabout, Clint thought. *Twice. The killer coming and the killer going – but why that far away?*

He thanked Salvador and sat to talk with him for a few minutes. He was more than average bright. He observed everything around, without commenting upon it, unless asked. Clint asked who was the killer. Did he have an opinion?

"I have what I think, but it may be wrong and for the wrong reasons."

So he wouldn't tell what it was. The Indios are like that. They're perfectly well aware that they would tend to think a certain person was the killer, simply because they didn't like that person. There was no one here he would tend not to like because everyone was trying to get along.

It would be the natural culture clash between the Indios and the blacks. Salvador was aware of that. He wouldn't say anything against them, unless he had very solid proof.

He went back to the car and talked with Judi. She agreed the Indios wouldn't speak against the blacks. They knew they didn't get along with them. The fact those were from Colon added to that.

"The blacks don't have any such thing," she said. "Elena keeps saying it has to be the Indios. They're that kind of people. I told her it was blacks from Colon who had that reputation, she knew it was mostly not true, but she does the same thing to the Indios. It goes a mile over her head."

"Tell me about it! People and their prejudices are the same everywhere and all the time. The Spanish will be sure it's the gringos. The gringos will probably be the only ones who don't have an opinion. They know it's prejudice. All they want to do is get out of here to finish their vacations."

"I want to get out of here, myself. It doesn't have anything to do with vacations. It's got a lot to do with dead bodies. Everything was so good until Santamaria's body was found, now it's all suspicion and fear. All of us. We know there's a killer, maybe a psycho, among us. It could be almost anyone."

"Don't say anything to anybody, but it's down to three."

She looked thoughtful, then nodded. "You won't say who they are, huh?"

"One of them. Somebody from outside." She gave him the finger. That was the most unlikely of all the possibilities. If anyone was anywhere in the area, they would know about it. The Indios, in particular, would know in minutes,

Clint strolled toward the bus, thinking. There might be

something on that bus that they missed. Something in a place where it would seem to be natural. There was a nagging that he had seen or heard something.

What?

He sat on a large boulder that had rolled onto the edge of the road to think. What had he seen? What was nagging at him?

He closed his eyes and mentally went through everything about that bus. The laptop. The memory sticks.

It had something to do with that laptop. He got the nag, when he thought about it.

Okay. They found the laptop case with no laptop, only some cell phones and chargers.

Not the laptop! The case! Those chargers! One was a standard type that would work with most cellulars here. The other was a fancy thing that only fit certain expensive types. Usually only one model.

So? Did that mean a cellular phone was missing? He hadn't found anything among them that was out of the ordinary here. No expensive ... but there was that one man using a satellite phone. He said there was no signal, but Clint was sure he was talking into it.

It was Santamaria. The nag was that his satellite phone was not among those found. He had called out. He did have a signal.

Did he contact his killer? Was there someone else following that bus who was close on the other side of the mudslide? Could someone have actually simply climbed over the slide and come here to kill him? Then why Sucha?

Same reason. He saw something. The Whiteface monkeys were disturbed when he was going back, or something.

It didn't quite fit. There was more that he didn't know then that he did. These side-trips did bring things back, like that satellite phone. He knew better than to begin to believe they were more than open speculation

He went on to the bus. That phone could have been anywhere and would have probably not been noticed, to any extent. He had lists of what was found in the luggage still on the bus, though it wasn't at all likely it was there.

He had lists of what was in the luggage at the culverts. It would be there and he probably would have noticed it at that time. The problem was that it could be put in a pocket or stuck behind a rock or put in a bush until that search was done. That was an item too easy to hide.

He went through the things from the initial search that were still on the bus. Cecilio said only three people had come to get their things. He had stayed right with all of them while they got whatever it was, mostly toothpaste and shaving things and fresh underwear. Two were the gringo and his wife and the third was Robnson for underwear and his notebook.

A search of the bus didn't turn up anything new. He did find a short list of phone numbers, international, in the Santamaria papers. It had his satellite phone's number on top. If he had another, he could call it and see whose pack it rang in.

Yeah! Right! They wouldn't have turned it off, first thing!

He went back to the culvert and said he was going to walk to where they were fixing the road to see how long it would be. Several people decided to walk with him, so they made a little parade. Salvador walked beside him on the left and Estevez on the right. They chatted about various things. The weather was really unusual this year.

It was getting worse every year.

Clint had his cellular in his pocket. When they walked over a little bridge over a stream it made a slight noise. It was the alert that there was a signal. He took out the cell and called Dave, his nutty musician friend. Dave was in Chiriqui Grande and would be in Bocas in the afternoon. He'd water and care for Judi's and Clint's flowers. Clint told him about what was going on.

He then called the national police and reported the murders and some of what he'd found.

His cellular was Movistar. Two others got the signal and called out. Mas Movil didn't get a signal and Claro didn't, at that spot.

They went on to watch the equipment moving the mud, putting it into large haulers to dump where there was another serious washout about to happen. It would be used to shore up the cut below the road and a concrete retainer built to hold it there. This mudslide would be used to stop a washout. Very efficient. It would be about ten hours before the road was passable.

Clint had surreptitiously inspected above the mud. He had no way to be certain, but it didn't look like a way across was likely, up there. Someone could have gone onto the ridge or other side of the mountain, but that wouldn't leave enough time to get to the bus – unless there was a path someone knew about that they didn't.

They returned to the culverts with the news. They stopped to make a call or two at the one small spot there was a signal. The signal died while they were talking. That could have been for any number of reasons.

Salvador was actually a better conversationalist than Estevez, who had dropped back. Penny Goodson's Spanish was poor, but she managed to talk with him, Clint filling in the spaces, both ways.

They got back to the culverts and told everyone the road would be open in about ten hours. They had called back and forth to the workers on the road crew and a bus would be there to take them back to Chitre as soon as they could get a path that was reasonably safe to walk across. They could bring their things to this side and be ready to cross when the path was open. It would be crossable in five to six hours. They couldn't make it faster because the wet mud kept sliding down as they dug for the path.

There wasn't much else to do. The fact that they might be able to make calls at the spot on the way added to the desire to get there and be ready.

Clint drove the car to the bus, where everyone got their luggage and packed it in. The surfboards were on top, wrapped in a blanket. The car was packed tight. He drove to the spot on this side of the mud and waited for them to walk up an hour later to each claim what was theirs. He then went back with the Indios to get their produce, what was left. Clint noticed that Salvador did as much as any of them, carrying heavy sacks of yuca and onions that very few gringo kids his age would even consider. They had everything there and covered with the tarp from the culverts when the light drizzle got a bit heavier. There was enough room for them to crowd under the tarp with Judi, Clint, Silvestre, Salvador and Ana Ricardo inside the car. It wasn't very comfortable, but wasn't uncomfortable. The close togetherness suited the Indios well, but the Sandros family started complaining about everything. Soon they were by themselves. No one would even speak to them. It wasn't Panamanian to complain about things when everyone was in the same fix. You tried to make things better, not worse.

Clint got out and went to them when Robinson came to say there was going to be trouble if they didn't stop acting like the world owed them more than the others. He told them to stop acting like they were from Colon. If they looked around, they could see that everyone was in the same situation. It wasn't pleasant for anyone – though everyone but them were trying to make the best of it. They got sullen and gave him hard looks. He gave them as hard looks back. He went back to the car.

He thought a lot about the murders. He couldn't figure it, unless someone came from outside. He was sure no one had. He wanted to solve this thing before these people could cross that mudslide and go. He had about two and a half more hours. It wasn't looking like he could pull it off.

Salvador was asleep. He hadn't slept last night. Things were under control, so he could relax a bit. That Silvestre was proud of the way his son was acting was as obvious as anything could be.

Judi gave Clint a look and slightly tossed her head. She wanted to talk to him, privately, so they got out and went a little way from the car.

"Clint, you have to tell me who the real suspects are. I can figure who aren't on the list, definitely, but have to know who is. I know you won't let your opinion enter into it. I'll treat it as confidential.

"You went up above that mud. You were looking for a way for someone to come across. That means you were serious when you said it could be someone from outside. It was also obvious you didn't find a way across. What's going on, now?"

"Santamaria carried a satellite phone that's missing. He called someone, so I felt it might have been someone following us who didn't get to the mud until it was already across the road. I have to find who has that phone. That one's the killer. It could only be two people."

"Santamaria's dead, but so is Sucha. Why?"

"He saw or heard something that would give the killer away, I suppose."

"Like that satellite phone in someone else's hand after Santamaria was killed?"

"Uh-huh."

"So. You won't tell me who because it would put me in a bad spot. I'll try to find if anyone saw a very expensive phone in anyone else's hands."

"That's about it. I have to find some way to identify the killer in less than two hours. I won't be getting anything more than I have, right now. That, as the saying goes, ain't good!"

"That's part of being in hell. I want out of here for a nice long shower and some good sound sleep. If anyone breathes too heavy or snores or just turns over in their sleep, I'm suddenly wide awake."

"Welcome to the club."

Clint couldn't help but feel that satellite phone was the key to solving this mess. He had an idea there was a number or two in storage on it that would tell him what was going on. His problem was that he had no effective way to find it.

He did have one idea. He said a few words to Judi, then started walking up the road toward the culverts. He held his breath as he approached the spot he found a signal before. There was a signal, but it was weak. The legend said emergency calls only.

That might do! He punched 999 and waited. There was no response. He punched 103 and the fire department came on. He identified himself and said he had reported a murder to the police, but the signal was too weak to get an answer. This one worked. All he wanted was for a call to be made. It was to a satellite phone. The phone was missing. The murderer might have it. There were people where they could hear if it rang. Please call the number.

There was a weak reply he couldn't quite make out, so he said the signal was fading and gave the number again.

Then he headed back. There had been no ringing from any of the packs or anywhere else.

He thought for a minute, then headed back to the bus in the car – with passengers.

Cecilio had heard a phone ringing in the bus. It stopped by the time he got there. Clint had him place as closely as he could the area of the call. About mid-bus.

He searched carefully, but found nothing. He was thinking literally of taking the bus apart, screw by screw, when it rang again. Above his head. He checked and found it was coming from a speaker. (The buses have speaker systems that they used to play music on the trips.) Clint pushed up on the speaker and it moved aside just enough for him to see the phone. He twisted the speaker around enough to reach it and took it to slip into his pocket, then put the speaker back in place. He then went to the car and was getting in as the phone buzzed again. He answered. It was the fire department. He said they found the phone. Thanks more than it was possible to say. It might mean a killer would be caught before he could get away. The Indios were chattering and Judy was grinning.

Clint went through the stored numbers, noting the ones that had been called since the last erase. There were only four. One had been called three times. The last three calls.

Clint called it. When it was answered with, "Licenciada Mary Castillo, como se ... oh, alo Guillermo. Que pasa?" he hung up.

So. The killer was Guillermo Robinson. Cecilio reported that he came to get his shaving kit and some underwear. He had hidden the phone, then. He left it there when they got the rest of their stuff because he was never in the bus alone, then. He probably figured that it would be found, eventually, but he could be long gone and there wouldn't be a way to connect him to it.

"Know who it is?" Judy asked.

"Oh, yeah!"

"One of the three?"

"Oh, yeah!"

Clint looked at his wristwatch. It would cut it awfully close. He hoped to get back before the path was opened.

He didn't make it. The path was opened and most of the people had left on the waiting bus to go back to Chitre. It would be another hour or more before he could get his car through.

He used the satellite phone to call the police and identify himself. He said to stop that bus and get Guillermo Robinson off. He was prime suspect in two murders. He must not be allowed to escape.

Now Clint could wonder what it was about, but he had an idea. Guillermo was selling a large property. He had been caught in some kind of fraud or other and was trying to get some kind of deal done that he could use to get away with a lot of money. Santamaria had found out about it, but had let Robinson know he knew. Robinson had killed him, then Sucha had seen him somewhere or with something, probably the satellite phone. He had confronted him, probably demanding to know why he didn't let the others know he had the thing.

That wasn't right, but it might not be too far wrong. All Clint could do now was wait and hope the police got Robinson off the bus. If he reached Chitre, he could disappear for a short while. They had his ID and information, so there was little doubt he would be found before long, even if he went into hiding.

The road was open in slightly less that an hour. They headed for Chitre. The Indios were delivered to the bus station to get their stuff. The murder bus and Sucha's body would be taken directly to the police impound and searched, minutely. Clint went by there and gave them the downloaded photos. He'd taken more than fifty more with his own camera when he was alone where the others wouldn't know.

Robinson had gotten off the bus before it was stopped. He was close to the secondary road that went to Divisa. Either he was heading for his property or he was trying to make them think he was. Clint decided to give it a day or two to cool down, then he would go after Robinson, if the police hadn't rounded him up by then. They were efficient, so would probably bring him in, soon.

He and Judi took the main road this time. They headed for Santiago. She would go to Bocas Town from there, Clint would try to find that lawyer. Mary Castillo. Santiago was as likely a place as any, but she was listed as being in Chitre.

Clint sat back to think. She had gotten those calls after Santamaria was dead and had that number on her numbers listing under Robinson's name. That was the only possible way she could have known who it was who was calling.

So. She was in on the scam – minimum.

He thought of something else, and grinned a small tight grin. He called Judi and said he was on his way back to Chitre. He could have thought of something before Santiago and saved himself eight hours of driving.

"What?"

"I think there's another little detour in this mess," Clint answered. "Something's added up."

"Such as?"

"Such as a lawyer knowing who was calling from a cell phone taken from a murdered man's belongings at the time of the murder."

"Yech! I see!"

"See you in Bocas. Just don't know when."

"I'll be waiting to hear the whole sordid thing about our trip to hell."

"Sordid. Brother, does that fit!"

He rang off, sighed deeply, cleaned up, changed clothes, swore a lot, got the tank filled and headed for Chitre. He'd stop for the night in Santiago. He'd been driving for seven hours, already, and would definitely need the break in four more.

It was raining a bit, which didn't make driving easy in the mountains, but Clint was so used to it he hardly noticed. He was in Santiago in a little under four hours, where he stopped at the Bocas del Toro Hotel, slept for six hours (His usual sleep time, even after an adventure like this), ate a good hearty breakfast and was on the road again. The Willie Nelson song kept going through his head. He would have liked to know what kind of car Robinson might be driving so he could check on whether he was heading for Santiago. He would most likely head for Panamá City to be able to hide among the over-population in a major city. Santiago wouldn't serve at all, and David wasn't that populated, either.

He got an idea before he reached Chitre and stopped in a small puebla not far away to don a disguise he used that he liked. He would become Donald Harrison, a man who would look like possibly a relative of Clint Faraday, but would be shorter and a little heavier (to the eye) and would walk and talk differently. That car wouldn't do. Robinson had been in it.

Clint paid the auto storage lot there $3.00 per day and took a bus into Chitre. He wouldn't rent a car there, unless it became absolutely necessary.

It took about two hours to locate the lawyer's office, which was in a private house just a few minute's walk from downtown. She wasn't there for the day. She would return tomorrow afternoon, according to the sign on the door. She specialized in real estate and immigration.

That would be how she met Williams. Clint remembered that conversation. He would be someone who had a residency through her. She would handle property titles and such for him. He might not be hard to find, if he lived in or near Chitre. The name would probably find him. Santamaria would have been in the Chitre area to investigate the property. That, alone, would make it probable he was there.

The way to find a gringo living in that kind of place was to simply ask the natives. It would be perfectly logical that a gringo in town would know about other gringos there and would like to visit. The best place was in a local bar gringos frequented.

Clint asked a taxi driver where the most popular gringo bar was. He was taken to a semi-fancy place that would be more expensive than others and wouldn't have anything to offer, other than the fact the gringos went there. The place was better than he'd expected and the drinks were only a little more than the average. They served food that had a good reputation, so he ordered a ribeye steak. It wasn't the best he'd ever tasted, but was fairly good. A little tough, but meat was tough in most places in Panamá. The yuca was fried in garlic butter, so was very good.

There were two Williams who came in every so often. Maybe once a week. One was a negro and one was white. They were both average popular. The black was in his thirties and the white was in his sixties. The black had a boat that took people out for fishing. The white studied animals for some book he was writing or something. He had written one that was sold at the universities. It was about animals that lived in or near water. He also wrote specialty articles for the English-speaking tourists about what to avoid or do to prevent denge, leichmeniasis, and so forth. The black was there two years ago for several months and had been back this time for two months, already. The white had been there three years.

It would be the white on a land scam. The black owned

a boat and lived aboard. He wouldn't be interested in any large plot of land, though Punta Arenas was on the water. Robinson's finca was supposed to be in Arenas.

Maybe he'd have to go to Arenas to see what was going on there and trace back. The only reason he was interested in that end of the deal was because the types who pulled land scams would concentrate on people like Williams, who were probably living on a pension and had some money saved over years to invest. It was a serious problem in Panamá that wasn't treated as such. The corruption in land deals was unbelievable. Each president who came along promised to do something about it, some did little things, most did nothing, so it went on and on. Dave, Clint's nutty musician friend, had been caught in that kind of deal and had learned enough to help Clint find those kinds.

He was sidetracked. His focus was to be on Robinson and Castillo, for the moment. He wasn't going to change the corrupt system overnight. He probably wouldn't be able to change it in his lifetime.

It was Thursday night. The more likely time for either Williams would be Friday or Saturday nights. Clint could spend the following day tying up details. He could go to the police station and check ... no, he couldn't. He was in disguise.

He called and got filled in on everything that had happened. Not much. They had found a woman near where Robinson got off the bus who had seen a man waiting near the road, but back in the trees. A car had stopped and he had gotten in. It left, heading toward Divisa. It was a new dark gray car. She didn't know or care about make and model. It was a car. A new one.

The police were quietly checking out everything around

Divisa. So far, only one person had seen what might have been them. Two men and a woman, the woman driving, had filled their tank at the bombas. It was a Nissan, 2009, two door, Sentra. Silver-gray and black.

Clint told them what he'd found, then hung up and sat back.

Divisa. Either they were seen at the logical place they would be seen going through or they were leaving a trail that would make it appear they were going through. They might go back to Chitre or go to Santiago or Panamá City. If they came there to divert the police, it would buy them time. All they needed was a day to get something set up in Panamá City. Castillo would return, after being gone for less than two days.

It would be Panamá City. It would also be very difficult to root him out in Panamá City.

Clint thought about it, then grinned. He went back to store his car and caught the bus for Arenas. That would be the last place they would expect him to go and the best place to find a connection. Maybe he could do a bit of diversion, himself!

Donald Harrison would come to Arenas in a truck driven by an old Indio named Lorenzo Betas. Clint knew him from several years ago and had been invited to come to his finca, anytime. He would always be a welcome guest. He was the man who saved the life of Lorenzo's son, Lucas, in Santiago, when some crooks tried to mug him – using a machete.

Clint drove the older rented car into the Betas' finca. He'd never been anywhere close to this place. He liked the scenery and the place. The Pacific could be seen about half a kilometer away toward the north. It looked very inviting and tranquil, from this distance.

Lorenzo and his wife came out to hug Clint and welcome him to their modest abode, in a manner of speaking. No disguise would work with the Indios, Clint had found. They recognized him almost immediately. They asked why he was disguised.

The home didn't look like much from outside, but was clean and comfortable inside, and quite nice, really. The Indios aren't into ostentation and aren't trying to impress anyone or compete with the Joneses. They want a clean, comfortable, efficient home. A place to enjoy your family and to relax. They are homes, not just houses.

Clint spent a time looking over the place. It was beautiful and peaceful. Lorenzo had four cows, two pigs, numerous chickens, two horses, corn, yuca, otoe, beans of several varieties, nance, guayabana, guavas, avocados, moronón (cashew) – just about everything he needed for himself, his family and a number of the poorer neighbors.

That's the Indio way. He had, so he shared with those who didn't have. In return, they would give him things he didn't have and would work their asses off to help him with the farm. He didn't like a couple of them and they didn't like him, but that had nothing to do with them helping each other. They may beat hell out of each other Saturday night, but would be back at working together on Monday. Clint was understanding more and more about the Indio way of life. He loved the people and he loved most of their lifestyle. They would stop to chat with everyone who was working that day, then move on.

Robinson's finca was about three kilometers east. It wasn't much. He'd been trying to sell it for years. The description was excellent, but the buyers would leave almost immediately when they saw it. Lorenzo took Clint out to a small island that was considered part of his property to point out the place to him. It had a lot of small islands out from it and was a very rocky small peninsula that was only about a foot or so above the waterline at high tide. At low tide, it looked very nice, from that distance, with beautiful patches of white beach between the points of rocks.

"There is no water at low tide. It is maybe six or eight centimeters deep where there are no rocks. The sand is only for a little bit, then it is more rocks. The bushes and other things make it very difficult to get to the water at all. The land can't be farmed, except in small patches. There are too many rocks and cattle will break their legs. There is little where a plant can make roots. It is not a good place. The Robinsons are not good people. They are not honest, so the rest of us will not stay silent when they try to get money from others for the land that is not worth anything."

"There's someone named Williams who's thinking of buying the land," Clint said. "I'm investigating. I think Guillermo Robinson killed two people. He's working with a crooked lawyer-cum-real-estate-agent in Chitre."

Lorenzo nodded. He said that was about what could be expected from such people. Clint could expect full cooperation with almost anyone here. Certainly with his people.

Then he showed Clint things to change in his disguise. Only the Indios would notice, but Robinson was mostly Indio. It was simple little things and surprised Clint with how much it was effective. He remembered a time in Puerto Armuelles when an Indio friend saw through his disguise from fifty feet away. It was because his hands were different when he took off the little ring he often wore or something Clint never understood. Lorenzo said that was obvious. The ring would distract from seeing the little scar on his thumb and would hide the way the veins crossed just before the fingers on the backs of his hands. He then showed Clint how differently the vein pattern was on his hands. Two others there showed their hands. Clint could just barely make out the pattern. It looked as distinctive as a fingerprint, when he trained himself to see it.

Lorenzo showed him how to use a very small bit of darker pigment from some handy clay to change the pattern to the eye. The clay would make a different pattern and was the same slight shading as his veins, and that was just one of several things they would notice without even being aware of using any such means of identification! It was automatic with them. He could wear sunglasses to hide the pattern of his retina. He knew about that, but his personal notice wasn't ten percent of what was automatic with the Indios.

When Clint left to go to the Robinson farm, he looked exactly the same from sixty or seventy feet, but was very different closer – in ways gringos and the Spanish and mixed Panamanians wouldn't notice. Clint didn't look like Clint to even them, when they finished showing him the tricks.

A photo wouldn't show anything different, at all, unless

you used a magnifying glass and knew what to look for.

Clint wondered if a program could be made for computers that would find those features in a photograph and could positively identify anyone, anywhere.

Probably! There was already far too much intrusion into peoples' lives by the agencies that surveyed them now. Screw it!

He said his goodbyes and promised to come visit again. He really meant that! He would definitely come back to this place. It was as much a paradise as some of the other places he'd visited.

Panamá was paradise, to Clint, but these places were special places in a special place. He rented a car in Arenas and drove to the gate that had a sign that said, "Se vende" and had the phone number of the owner or real estate agent. He called it and was told there was no one available to show the place, at this time, but he had permission to go in as he pleased. There was an apology because the road only went in a short way and not to the coast. Clint said he would look over what he could from the road and thanked the woman for her time.

He went in and parked at the end of the little road. It was no more than fifty meters inside and ended surrounded by small scrub trees. He could see over in spots and all he saw was the scrub for a few meters, then the land dropped and he could see the ocean about 600 meters past. He couldn't see much through the scrub, but a person would assume it was the same as this small area. Good solid land, just covered with the scrub.

There were large trees in the area. A lot of them, but this was only scrub?

Clint dug up some of the soil. It wasn't the type by the road. This was filled.

Okay. They had filled a few meters close to the road and planted that scrub that would grow so dense you couldn't get through without a way to cut a path. Where the land dropped was where the original was. It was steep enough that you couldn't see what it was like through that scrub. People would assume it was the same as what they drove past.

There was a small break to one side where someone had cut a path, at one time. Clint had a machete in the car, so he re-cut the path that led through the scrub to a rocky slope down to the ocean. It was obvious from there that the land was worthless and the shore was worse. The tide was low enough that he could see nothing but rocks with small puddles between them to the islands, which were covered with mangroves that no one could cut. It would make a nice picture of a rocky Oregon coast with mangroves, but wasn't useful for anything at all. Clint went on along the rocks. He didn't see anything more.

Did Williams make that cut? If so, why was he still interested in this land? What about it gave it any value, at all, except as a bird preserve or something.

Now he had a real puzzle! – unless Williams didn't make that cut. Did Santamaria?

That was something to consider. Santamaria found something that would show Williams the land was worthless. He had died, as a result.

He took pictures from all angles he could for as much of it as he could, got in the car, and headed back to Arenas.

He decided to find what he could that the people in the town knew. The Indios kept out of it, didn't like the Robinsons, and didn't know much about any business deals. The other people knew that the Robinsons were trying to sell the place and weren't having any success.

Most of them were more or less neutral about the family, but some didn't like them, at all. He didn't find anyone who actually did like them. They knew some gringo was interested in the land and had come there several times, once with a university professor named Guerra. Doctor Guerra. He thought he was smarter than anyone. They didn't like him, but that was his purpose. The type wouldn't mix with the normal people, only with other professors and politicians.

"Yeah. A real pain in the ass type? Better than anyone?" Clint asked Gloria, the pretty waitress.

"Better than god, if you accepted his attitude," she agreed. "We get some, but most are just gringos being gringos." She had a sparkle in her eyes as she said it.

"Yeah, we don't just think we're better, we *know* we are!"

"Some of you are fun. Some are, as you said, pains in the ass. People are people, no matter where they come from. Guerra is Panamanian."

"Does the Castillo woman come here much?"

"Castillo?"

"Bienes raices. Real estate agent."

"In the fancy silver car? A few times. She's a crook you can smell from ten kilometers away. She doesn't know how to act any different than a crook. Her father was the same. He came before her to find land to sell around here. If you're raised by pigs you'll act like a pig."

Clint liked her. She had a good sense of humor. "Are you married or seeing anyone special?" he asked.

"No and no. I get off work at six, when the other girl comes on duty."

"I'll be here. Do you know any good places to go?"

"Two. That's all we have."

"Okay. We can try them both. Do you know of a good restaurant?"

She laughed. "This is as good as we have."

"It'll do. Six o'clock."

He hadn't planned to stay the night, but what the hell? He hadn't planned *not* to, either! She was a bit younger than most of the girls he dated, not being more than twenty five, but she was the one who suggested it and she was great looking with a great personality. Why not?

He spent the rest of the afternoon, after booking into the one hotel he'd seen, meeting people and chatting about anything that came up. About four, he went back to Lorenzo's finca and told him he was staying in town tonight. It was business, so he couldn't be at Lorenzo's home, much as he would prefer that. He didn't want them to think he chose to do that. The Indios would wonder if they had done something to make him choose not to stay with them. They were sensitive and would worry that they'd said or done something to offend him. Coming to explain made it plain that he wasn't there because of other things, not because of anything they'd done.

His night was great. Gloria was a lot of fun and knew everyone in town, it seemed. She was popular. Several men told him they would give up limbs if she would take them seriously, but she was determined to wait for some man who wouldn't treat her like cattle if they got serious. She knew men and she was smart. She wasn't pretending to like the gringo because gringos always had so much money. She wasn't impressed by that type.

That made him feel good. He was used to having a good time with a woman, but nothing serious. It was fun with someone he could care about. He liked to sing "What's love got to do with it?" when starting on a date to let them know it wasn't to go any further than fun, unless that developed naturally from getting to know each other.

Gloria was as frank and felt much the same. They got along far better than he would have expected.

They went to the two places she recommended, after having a good meal at the restaurant. Clint liked them both and liked most of the people he met there. He was very definitely coming back here as much as was reasonable and little enough that it wouldn't grow old and stale. This was like Cusapín. He doubted that it would grow stale if he was there permanently.

They went to his room for the night at twelve thirty. Almost everything in town shut down at eleven, at the latest, but they were in a small bar with good people. It stayed open later because the gringo was so popular.

He was going to have to get back to his case.

Tomorrow.

Gloria had to be at work at 6:30 and was a little worried he wouldn't want to get up that early. 5:30, so she could go home and change. He said he was always up before that, anyhow.

When she was gone, he went out front to find a place to get coffee. The only place was a small restaurant where the Indios went to get rides to work or to find someone who needed workers for one thing or another. He liked the place and he liked the coffee and he liked the people. Everything that happened made him like the place more.

He talked about anything that came up and put in little suggestive words or phrases the way Judi had taught him. He would get answers, that way, when the person who gave the answer wasn't aware he had said anything and where he would seem almost not to hear the answer. It was a disarming technique that put people off their guard from an unexpected angle.

The Robinsons weren't liked by other Indios. Williams was alright, but not too smart, they felt. Castillo was a crook, the same as her father had been.

They were jealous that Clint was with Gloria (good-natured) when they all tried. She would date some of them once or twice, but refused to get serious. They every one wanted to get serious with her. She wasn't Indio, but she thought and felt like an Indio. Her grandfather was a Cuna. It wasn't an act.

Clint had all he was likely to gain from being there. He hated to leave, but there was no point in staying – now. He would be back. He turned in the older car he'd rented and caught the bus for Santiago. It went through Divisa, so he'd pick up his own car there and head for ... where? Back to Santiago? David? Bocas? Panamá City?

He was still undecided when he got his car. He'd gotten rid of the disguise and was Clint Faraday again.

That's the trouble with having everything so good for a few days. It leaves you in a state where all you really want to do is go back.

He would drive to Santiago. The detour was fixed and open, so he wouldn't worry much about getting stuck again – though the rains were back to excessive and were getting worse. La Niña, they said. Maybe.

He was on the detour for about twenty kilometers and had noticed a car behind that seemed to stay a certain distance. He slowed, it slowed. He speeded up, it speeded up. He was being followed. All he could see about the car was that it was a silver-gray smaller car.

A Nissan Sentra?

He went around a curve awhile later and came to the spot where they had stayed in the culverts. He pulled off the road and waited until the silver-gray car came around the bend and saw him sitting there. They came to block his way out with their own car, which made him feel like an idiot. He knew better than to pull into a place where that was even possible!

He reached under the seat and took out his Glock. This might get hairy. This was the last time he'd ever take that detour – one way or another. He hoped he'd survive *to* take it!

Robinson got out of the car with a pistol in his hand. Clint brought the Glock to just below the window, where it would be ready and out of sight.

Robinson came closer, cautiously. A woman was sitting in the car. She might be armed, too. Clint would have to be ready to move fast. He tensed and waited, looking like he was relaxed and eating a snack (he had some hojaldres and a thermos full of coffee).

Robinson came to the window, pistol pointed at Clint's head. Clint grinned and pointed to the (phony) video-cam on the dash and said, "Smile! You're on Candid Camera!"

Robinson didn't get the reference. He shrugged and said, "So you have a recorder. It can be erased."

"Not if you can't get to the recorder. What do you want?"

"I want to know why you're interfering with my business here!"

"Because it goes so far beyond business when people start getting killed. I'd think even a stupid shithead like you could figure that!"

"They were going to cost me fifteen years of work!"

"Oh. Then it's alright. They deserved to die if they were going to expose some slimy sleazeball crook."

He looked exasperated. "Do you know how much money's involved here? What would *you* do?"

"God! Everyone who uses that question has to be a scumbag like you! I've heard it from ten people. All ten were the same damned kind of worthless slime! Money isn't everything, it's not even much.

"I wouldn't be trying to run a crooked scam, so I wouldn't do anything."

"I'm not going to let you get away with it! You don't leave me any choice!" He pointed the pistol directly between Clint's eyes. Clint looked over Robinson's shoulder and smirked. Robinson instinctively glanced back to see who was there. Clint shot him three times before he could turn back. The Nissan's tires spun on the gravel and it headed back toward Divisa.

Clint didn't have pictures of the encounter, but he had recorded it on a cassette recorder he carried. He got out and checked Robinson's body, finding the name and number of a Lawrence Williams, which he copied.

A bus came around the bend and Clint flagged it. He told the driver there was a dead body there. He'd been shot. As soon as he could find a signal, possibly just ahead by the ravine, call the police and report it. He'd wait for them there.

The driver looked scared and said he'd see it was reported now, if there was anyone the CB would reach. He tried and got a weak response. He explained and was told it would be reported, immediately.

The bus left. Clint sat on a culvert with a branch above to give some shade, and waited. The police truck came about an hour later. Clint identified himself and told them exactly what happened. They would get an alert out for Castillo and her Nissan. They had a radio and a relay vehicle, so it was done in seconds.

She had time to get to Divisa. That was the first place she could leave this road and find another that went anywhere else. They could trace every road out of Divisa she could have reached in an hour's time at the maximum speed she could go in that car in the mountains.

Clint stayed until they had everything he could help with wrapped up. They said he was acting with those police papers, so they wouldn't make him leave the gun with them. He might well need it again. He had established a very good reputation with the police.

Clint headed back toward Divisa. This would be the last trip on the detour through Hell! Things were so perfect everywhere else!

As soon as he could get a strong signal, he called

Williams. He got the voice mail and said to please call him on a matter of grave import as soon as he possibly could. He drove on. He was just getting to Divisa when Williams called. He told him some of what had happened and wanted to know if Williams knew that property was worthless. Robinson was dead.

"Where are you?" Williams asked.

"Divisa."

"I'm only a half hour away. I'll meet you there in forty five minutes. I have to finish this, but I'll come as soon as it's done. It's business, and the Robinson property is involved. Meet me at Yolanda's?"

"Which is where? I don't know Divisa."

"On the edge of town, heading toward Chitre."

"I think I've seen it. I'll be there."

Now all he could do was wait. He found Yolanda's and used the time to call Judi to give her an update on what was going on. Williams came in fifty minutes from the call, so he wasn't on Panamanian time. If he was, it would be at least three hours before he showed up. Clint was pointed to him as he came in. He came to the table and Clint said to bring two Balboas to the waitress and introduced himself. Williams introduced himself as Larry.

"So. What's it about? I've heard the land isn't worth anything, but that would depend on what you want to do with it."

"What do you want to do with it?"

"Let it sit for five to ten years, then turn it over for a big profit when the influx gets going good. There are a lot of people who want land like that. It's got a view and some coast with beaches, so it's got enormous potential.

"If I don't invest in something longterm, I'll throw the money away and end up broke, in a year or so. This'll force me to live within my means."

"There aren't any beaches there. The sand's out of the water at low tide and there's nothing there but slick rocks in the water that's only a few centimeters deep."

"So I've been told. A man was trying to get me to go out there with him before I signed anything or gave anyone any money. He said he would take me to where I couldn't deny he was telling the truth. He said there was something else about the property he was checking on.

"I had an engineer with credentials with the government out there. He looked over the charts and so forth the government has and said I can dredge my own channel up to ten meters wide and can use the sand to expand the beach there. It's a lot of rocks that don't serve much ecological purpose and that's protected by the shallows outside from washout.

"Santamaria. That was the one who was murdered on a bus or something. I remember seeing something about it on TV."

"He was murdered by Robinson. So was a man named Sucha, who had the bad fortune to see Robinson with Santamaria's fancy cell phone after Santamaria was dead. Robinson had a gun pointed at my head when he died. He allowed me one second when he was distracted. Castillo was driving him and got the hell out of there before I could get a shot at her."

Williams was staring at Clint in disbelief. "But ... but she ... I was with her when you called! She wanted me to put something down on the land. She said Robinson had another interested buyer who would pay more and she had a lot of time and money invested in the sale to me!"

"She wants money to be able to run. The police are after her ass, bigtime!" Clint took out his phone and called the police to report that she was in Divisa an hour ago. Williams told them where his place was and said she took the Las Tablas cutoff road. They would have her in fifteen minutes. There wasn't anywhere for kilometers where she could get off that road. They would call Clint the minute they had her. He could come to Divisa station to identify her and her car. Williams said he'd like to be along to find what was really going on. He'd given her five hundred dollars to hold the land. He had first refusal at the price already quoted.

They had another beer and waited until the call came that she would be at the station in ten minutes. The officer who called said she was the type that made cops want the right to smack them in the mouth. He was definitely going to report her for trying to bribe him with two hundred dollars to give her one-half hour to get away.

"Well, let's see what the hell this crap is really about!" Williams said. "It seems extreme. I knew most of what was wrong with the land and would've bought it, anyhow. I would've tried to get the price down more, but it was good enough for me, as it was."

They finished their beer and headed for the station.

"She's being entered now. She's a lawyer, so she's giving us one hell of a time quoting laws that don't apply to criminal cases," Javier, the police officer who brought her in, reported. "I would love the right to smack that one in the mouth a few times – and I don't believe in hitting a woman, for any reason! What a *bitch*!"

They chatted. Clint explained more about the bus and what he figured was happening. Much of it was confirmed. She was involved in a land scam that resulted in the murders and the attempt on his own life. Javier got the report on Santamaria to add what Clint found. "Did you know he had been checking the registro and catastro?" he asked.

"Who? Santamaria?"

"Yes. This may have some grave import on the murders and explain why Robinson was so adamant about keeping anyone else out of it. Mr. Williams has stated he knew that the land was considered worthless, but he had a plan. The state of the land wasn't very deeply involved in his decision – but problems with catastro and the registro could well mean it was about something more."

"Larry, let's go to catastro, right now! I have the authorization papers with the police to get me into those files, fast!"

"I will accompany you," Javier said. "If what I am suspecting eventuates, there is ten times the motive that a court would demand. It will make this a, as you gringos say about basketball, slam dunk!"

They headed for the public records department, where they checked on the Robinson land. It turned out the land was owned by Robinson's uncle. It had never changed registration, which meant the land legally belonged to a son of his uncle, since the uncle died in an accident six years ago. A Paulo Santana Robinson. A sale could be contested – successfully – at any time. The land wasn't legally Robinson's to sell.

"So. We know what Santamaria found," Javier said. "We have far more than enough motive for all of it. Castillo has to know about this. It is what a lawyer *does*. She will be part of the, as you call it, scam. She knew of this one day after agreeing to sell it."

"Yup!" Clint agreed. Williams nodded.

"Say! Does that thing have a way to get in touch with this Santana character?" Williams asked.

"Yes. It has an address, if an old one," Javier said. He gave him the address. In David

"Well! It looks like I'm heading for David! I might still want to buy it, if Santana wants to sell."

"He will," Clint said. "He doesn't even know he has it, it seems."

"Do not be too sure," Javier warned.

"Oh?" Williams replied.

"I see," Clint said. "His name and number are on those papers. It could be that he's in on the scam. Sell it to you for a fairly cheap price, Robinson and Castillo go somewhere with the money, then Santana makes a claim. He knows about the land being his from those records, right there."

"Phew!" from Williams.

"Still want to go? You may have him in a spot where he has to sell it to you damned cheap to stay out of serious charges, himself," Clint pointed out.

"I'm not interested in any forced or crooked ... but they were trying to do that to me! Let's get this boat in the water! Your car or mine?"

"I'm going there, anyhow. Mine."

They finished the business with the police, Larry went home to get some clothes and so forth, Clint had another beer, then they were on the way to David.

"Mr. Santana? I'm Lawrence Williams. I was going to buy your property in Arenas. Robinson is dead and Castillo is in the pen. It's your land, and I want it. How much?

"Figure your cut of what they were going to scam me out of and I'll pay that for it as soon as it's registered in my name. Título."

"Título? I think not."

"Then you don't think at all," Clint said. "Clint Faraday. Police and private detective, acting as private detective here, but it could become police, with a word."

"Er?"

"It was a scam that resulted in three people dying. If you don't make the sale, it shows your complicity, therefore your guilt, in the scam and murders. Simple," Williams said.

"Six to ten years," Clint agreed.

Santana sat down. Hard. He stuttered a bit, but didn't quite say anything.

"Well?!" Williams demanded. "How much? I'll see if I want to spend that or if I'll wait for your conviction and buy it from the government for thirty two cents a meter. Titled!"

"Thirty cents a meter and you get the title. I'll sign the papers with a notary."

Williams raised an eyebrow at Clint, who nodded the slightest bit.

"I'll have to think ... but I want to do this today, so I can get back to Divisa. Twenty six cents. That will make it cost about what they were going to charge."

"WHAT!!" he screamed. "They were going to sell it for sixty cents a meter?! They told me they were getting forty cents!"

"They were crooks. You were one, too. You believed them?" Clint asked. "You would split thirds, huh?"

He nodded.

"Give him twenty cents a meter. He comes out better than he would have. So do you." Clint said to Williams. "He was going to scam you out of a little, himself."

"I would have had the land back to sell again!" he

protested.

"There would never have been a second deal after you tried it once," Williams pointed out. "I'll split the difference. Twenty three cents."

Santana nodded and gave him a sickly grin. They went to the catastro and got in just before it closed for the day. They would have to finish it tomorrow, but Clint wasn't needed, anymore. He arranged for a law firm he knew to handle it. He warned Williams of what lawyers were like – as Castillo should have shown him. Take care!

"*That*, I can promise you!" he replied.

Clint soon headed back to Bocas. On the main road. No more detours. They had a way of turning sour on him.

"So that was about it. He got the land, titled, cheaper than they were going to sell it to him for. It's worthless, now, but his plans might make him come out," Clint explained to Judi, as they drove toward Chiriqui Grande. "It was one hell of an experience, but I found a place I'll have to show you, sometime."

"I love everyplace you've taken me to meet your Indio friends," she agreed. "We're going to Punta Peña, then to Chiriqui Grande, then to Cusapín to one of those places right now, so I'll love it. I always do."

"They're the real Panamá. I love this place more every day."

"I feel the same. Bocas grows stale, if you stay too long, but it's a great place for a base. We go all over the country from there."

"Uh-huh. Anyhow, Castillo got six years. We kept the agreement with Santana and didn't press any charges, but he knows we can, if he ever gets out of line again. He came out good."

"Oh! We're coming to the Valle de Aguas road! We can take a detour there, right to Punta Peña!"

Clint gave her the finger.

C. D. Moulton's works are available on most major outlets as printed or e-books. CD writes the CD Grimes, PI, mysteries, the Det. Lt. Nick Storie mysteries, the Clint Faraday mysteries, the Flight of the Maita science fiction series, books on orchid culture and many others of many types. Mystery, adventure, intrigue, science fiction, humor, fantasy, paranormal, mild erotica, and factual.

www.ingramcontent.com/pod-product-compliance
Lightning Source LLC
Chambersburg PA
CBHW052229150726

48002CB00003B/1337